Table of Contents

Rourke Educational Media

A Division of Carson Dellosa Education

rourkeeducationalmedia.com

Can you find these words?

graze

herd

predators

stripes

What Do Zebras Do?

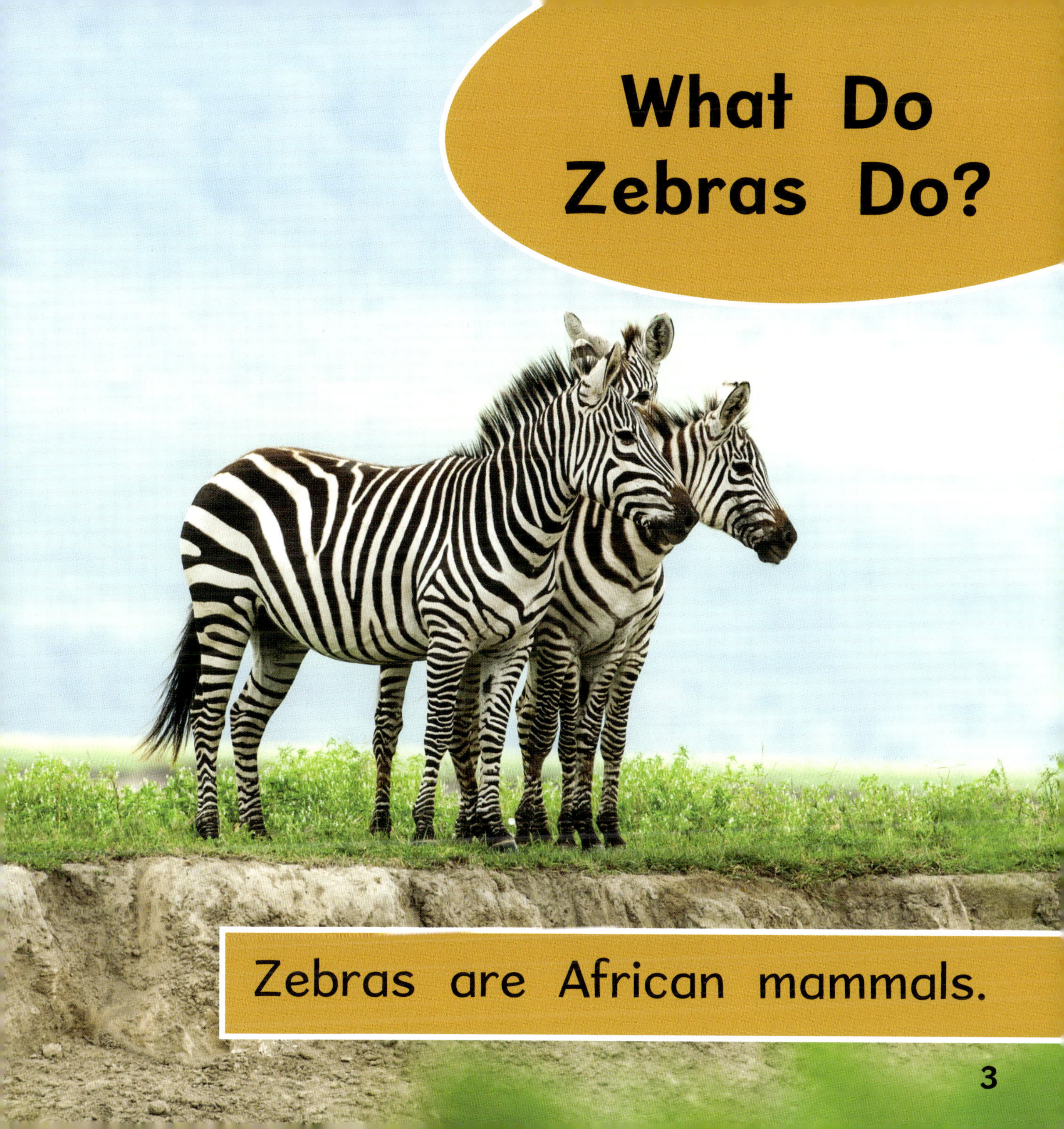

Zebras are African mammals.

Zebras **graze** on grass.

They eat only plants.

Zebras move!

They travel far to find food and water.

Zebras know each other.

Each has different **stripes.**

Zebras live together in a **herd**.

herd

Zebras fight **predators**!

They kick and bite.
They protect the herd.

Did you find these words?

Zebras **graze** on grass.

Zebras live together in a **herd.**

Zebras fight **predators**!

Each has different **stripes**.

Photo Glossary

graze (grayz): To feed on grass and other plants.

herd (hurd): A group of animals of one kind that stays together.

predators (PRED-uh-tuhrs): Animals that hunt and eat other animals.

stripes (strypes): Long bands of color.

Index

About the Author

Lisa Jackson is a writer from Ohio. She would like to visit Africa someday, especially to see its amazing animals. For now, she likes to feed the giraffes at the Columbus Zoo!

www.rourkeeducationalmedia.com

PHOTO CREDITS: Cover ©Kyslynskyy; Pg 2, 10, 14, 15 ©Delbars; Pg 2, 12, 14, 15 ©v_rybakov; Pg 2, 4, 14, 15 ©yod67; Pg 2, 8, 14, 15 ©jamenpercy; Pg 3 ©jrphoto6; Pg 6 ©GlobalP

Edited by: Keli Sipperley
Cover and interior design by: Rhea Magaro-Wallace

Library of Congress PCN Data
Zebra / Lisa Jackson
(African Animals)
ISBN 978-1-73160-559-7 (hard cover)(alk. paper)
ISBN 978-1-73160-445-3 (soft cover)
ISBN 978-1-73160-608-2 (e-Book)
ISBN 978-1-73160-682-2 (ePub)
Library of Congress Control Number: 2018967316

Printed in the United States of America,
North Mankato, Minnesota